for Alexandra

a min**e**dition book

Copyright © 2004 by Stephanie Roehe
Coedition with Michael Neugebauer Publishing Ltd. Hong Kong
All rights reserved. This book, or parts thereof, may not be reproduced in
any form without permission in writing from the publisher,
Penguin Young Readers Group,
345 Hudson Street, New York, NY 10014.
The scanning, uploading and distribution of this book via the Internet or
via any other means without the permission of the publisher is illegal and
punishable by law. Please purchase only authorized electronic editions,
and do not participate in or encourage electronic piracy of copyrighted
materials. Your support of the author's rights is appreciated.
Published simultaneously in Canada.
Manufactured in Hong Kong by Wide World Ltd.
Designed by Michael Neugebauer
Typesetting in Cafeteria
Color separation by Fotoreproduzioni Grafiche, Verona, Italy.

Library of Congress Cataloging-in-Publication Data available upon request.

ISBN 0-698-40004-6
10 9 8 7 6 5 4 3 2 1
First Impression
For more information please visit our website: www.minedition.com

"That's Not Fair!"

Stephanie Roehe

Translated by Charise Myngheer

"He has more than me!" shouted Fia as she jerked her brother's tail.

"That's not true!" Fabi argued.

"Then trade with me." Fia offered.

But Fabi didn't want to trade.

"See, Mom?" shrieked Fia. "He does have more!"

"Stop arguing right now!" demanded Mama Fox angrily.

"Or I'll eat both cookies myself!"

Fia thought that sounded like a dirty trick.

Fabi just laughed.

Fia gave her brother another quick kick.

And Mama Fox saw it all.

"I warned you," she said. "Now you have nothing to fight over."

And with two bites, the cookies disappeared in Mama Fox's mouth.

"It's your own fault," exclaimed Mama Fox.
"Why do you always have to fight over your food, anyway?"

"It's normal," they answered together. "That's what kids do."
Mama Fox shook her head in disagreement.
"Come with us, then. We'll show you!" Fabi challenged.
"But if we're right, we get two more cookies! Okay?"

"Okay," Mama Fox promised.

So Fia, Fabi, Mama Fox and Florina headed toward the Bear Family's house. When they reached the playground in the center of the forest, they decided to rest under a tree.

BINK! BONK! Something hit Mama Fox on her head! It was a nut!

They looked up and saw Mama Squirrel scolding Sally and Sulley. Sally got so nervous that she had dropped their dinner. Naturally, Sulley argued with Sally even louder after that.

"Did you hear that, Mom?" asked Fia. "Told you we were right! Everybody fights over food!"

"That's just one example. And one example is certainly not *everybody*," insisted Mama Fox. "It'll take more than that to convince me."

"Okay, we'll show you some more," said Fabi. "Come on!"

·13·

Mama Fox saw Mrs. Bear in the distance.
She didn't appear to be in a very good mood.
Then they heard little Bonnie crying.
Her brother had stolen her ice cream and was racing around the yard,
yelling, "Now it's mine. Now it's mine."

Before Mama Fox could get out of the way, Bonnie's ice cream
landed all over the front of her new dress.
"See, Mom?" Fia and Fabi chimed in together, "everybody
fights over food."
But Mama Fox still wasn't ready to give in.
"That's just two examples," she argued. "And
two examples aren't even close to *everybody!*"

As they continued along their way, they met Mr. Deer.
"My ears! My nerves! Deana and Derrin are always fighting! They even fight when they each get a whole loaf of bread," he complained. "I can't win!"

"They each get a whole loaf of bread?" questioned Fia in disbelief. "If I got so much bread, I'd never fight. I couldn't even eat a whole loaf of bread!"

Mama Fox groaned, "It does seem to be the same problem in every family."

"Good bye, Mr. Deer," she said with a wave. "Please stop by for a cup of coffee sometime."

"See, Mom? We told you. We were right!"
Mama Fox thought about giving in, but "Three examples aren't–"
Fia interrupted her. "All good things come in threes!" she exclaimed.
"Just accept it, Mom. We win!"
"And now you have to bake cookies for us," claimed Fabi excitedly.
"Okay, okay," Mama Fox agreed. "A promise is a promise.
Let's go home now."

Everybody helped.
Mama Fox chopped the nuts. Fabi stirred the dough.
Fia greased the baking sheet, and Florina watched everyone to be sure that nobody made a mistake.

The kitchen smelled delicious!
DING! Mama Fox carefully pulled the cookies out of the oven.

Fia and Fabi immediately grabbed a cookie and ran outside to play
in the garden.
"All's well that ends well," announced Fia.

"Yeah, all's well for you, anyway. This time you have more than me!"
complained Fabi.
"Do you want to fight again?" asked Fia. "Wait until I catch you!"
she threatened.
Fabi laughed and ran as fast as he could to get away from her.
Suddenly he tripped over a rock and fell to the ground.
His cookie flew through the air and over the hedge in front of him.

Before he could get up and start running again, Fabi saw two small mice sitting on a rock. They were sharing a teeny tiny kernel of corn.

"Why aren't you fighting over your corn kernel?" asked Fabi.

"Because it's all we have," answered Lina.

Fia and Fabi looked confused.

"If one of us eats the whole thing, then the other one would starve," Lina continued to explain.

"And if one of us starved, we wouldn't have anybody to play with," announced Lenni.

"I never thought about it that way," agreed Fabi. "Playing alone isn't fun."
"I could break my cookie into four pieces," Fia suggested sweetly.
"Good idea," agreed Fabi. And that's exactly what Fia did.

So Fia, Fabi, Lina and Lenni played together as they nibbled on their cookie pieces. They all agreed that it was the best cookie they had ever eaten.

They never found the cookie that Fabi lost. But it didn't really matter. They played together often and didn't think about it anymore.

Or maybe they did.